For my magical neighbors,
Rosario and Rita Macchione — CW

To my late uncle Marcel — LM

ROSARIO'S

Published in Canada and the USA in 2015 by Groundwood Books

Groundwood Books / House of Anansi Press
110 Spadina Avenue, Suite 801, Toronto, Ontario M5V 2K4
or c/o Publishers Group West
1700 Fourth Street, Berkeley, CA 94710

We acknowledge for their financial support of our publishing program the Canada Council for the Arts, the Government of Canada through the Canada Book Fund (CBF) and the Ontario Arts Council.

Library and Archives Canada Cataloguing in Publication
Wahl, Charis, author
Rosario's fig tree / written by Charis Wahl ; illustrated by Luc Melanson.
Issued in print and electronic formats.
ISBN 978-1-55498-341-4 (bound).--ISBN 978-1-55498-342-1 (pdf)
I. Melanson, Luc, illustrator II. Title.
PS8645.A44R68 2015 jC813'.6 C2014-905595-1
C2014-905596-X

The illustrations were done digitally.

Design by Michael Solomon
Printed and bound in Malaysia

FIG TREE

Charis Wahl

Pictures by Luc Melanson

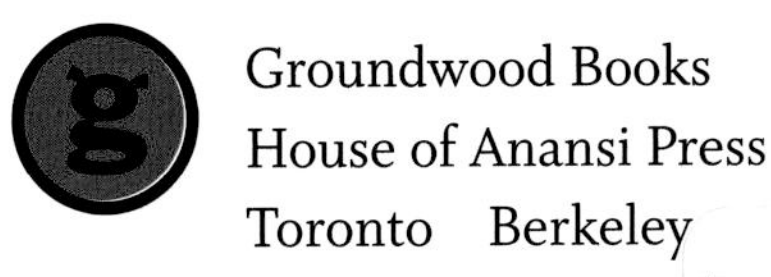

Groundwood Books
House of Anansi Press
Toronto Berkeley

ROSARIO lives next door.

He's a magician.

He doesn't pull rabbits out of hats or find pennies behind your ears.

He's a garden magician.

Here's how I know.

We have flowers in our garden. We have weeds, too, but some of them are pretty.

Rosario's garden is full of vegetables.

Every spring Rosario turns over the soil and gets it ready to grow things. He knows the perfect day to put in every plant and seed. It never snows or gets too cold after that.

I ask him how he knows the right day, but he just smiles. It must be a magician's secret.

I help on planting days. He tells me how big to make the holes. Some are as big as my hand. Some are as little as my baby finger.

All spring and summer Rosario grows tomatoes and peppers and beans and zucchinis and cucumbers and eggplants and lots of things I don't know.

Last spring he did a strange thing. One day he brought a big pot out of the house. It had a tree in it as tall as he is.

"It's a fig tree," he said. "At home we have fig trees everywhere. Here it's too cold for figs. But we'll see."

He took the tree out of the pot and planted it in a hole.

All summer the tree grew — big, wide leaves and then lots of purple figs. Rosario gave the figs to all his friends. I'm his friend, too.

Figs are kind of squishy, but they are as sweet as peaches.

In the fall, when it was getting cold, Rosario dug up all the vegetables. Soon there was nothing left in the garden except the fig tree.

"It's too cold for figs now," he said, and started digging. He made a long hole in front of the tree and put boards around the edges. Then he dug out just enough soil to loosen some of the roots.

"Now we bury it," he said, and bent the tree over, lower and lower, until it lay in the hole. "Good-bye, tree."

He put leaves all around it and plastic over the top. Then he shoveled in soil until you couldn't see that there had ever been a tree there.

I said we should have a funeral. Rosario just smiled. He didn't seem very sad, but I know he loved that tree.

All winter I thought about the tree. It had snow all over it, and the cold wind swooshed around the garden.

Did dead things feel lonely?

This spring, on the first planting day, Rosario's friends came over. They kept telling him things to do.

But Rosario is a magician. He doesn't need help!

He dug holes for the tomato plants. I pushed in the stakes for the beans to climb. He planted radicchio and potatoes. I sprinkled the seeds for the radishes.

50L

Then he started digging where the grave was.

What was he doing?

Did he forget about the tree?

I tried to stop him, but his friends just patted me on the head.

"Don't worry, little one," they said. "It's okay."

Off came the soil and the plastic and the dead leaves. But the tree lay still and dead.

Rosario bent down, put his arm around the trunk and slowly made it stand up. It looked like he wanted to dance with his tree. Then he put soil all around the trunk.

His friends cheered, but I didn't.

It was creepy. The tree was standing up, but it was still dead.

Every day I watched Rosario's garden.

The tomato plants got taller, the radicchio poked its purple leaves out of the soil, the beans climbed their stakes. But the tree just stood there.

Yesterday it started to be summer.

"Just like home today," Rosario said. "Beautiful. Blue sky, hot sun. Come, look."

And there it was — a new green leaf on the fig tree.

"You are a magician, Rosario," I said.

"No magic," he said. "You just learn, and then you know."

And I know Rosario's a magician.
For sure.